Good Night, Little Dragons

By Leigh Ann Tyson
Illustrated by Jim Bernardin

 A GOLDEN BOOK · NEW YORK

Library of Congress Control Number: 2011924177
Educators and librarians, for a variety of teaching tools, visit us at www.randomhouse.com/teachers
ISBN: 978-0-307-92957-0
Printed in the United States of America
10 9 8

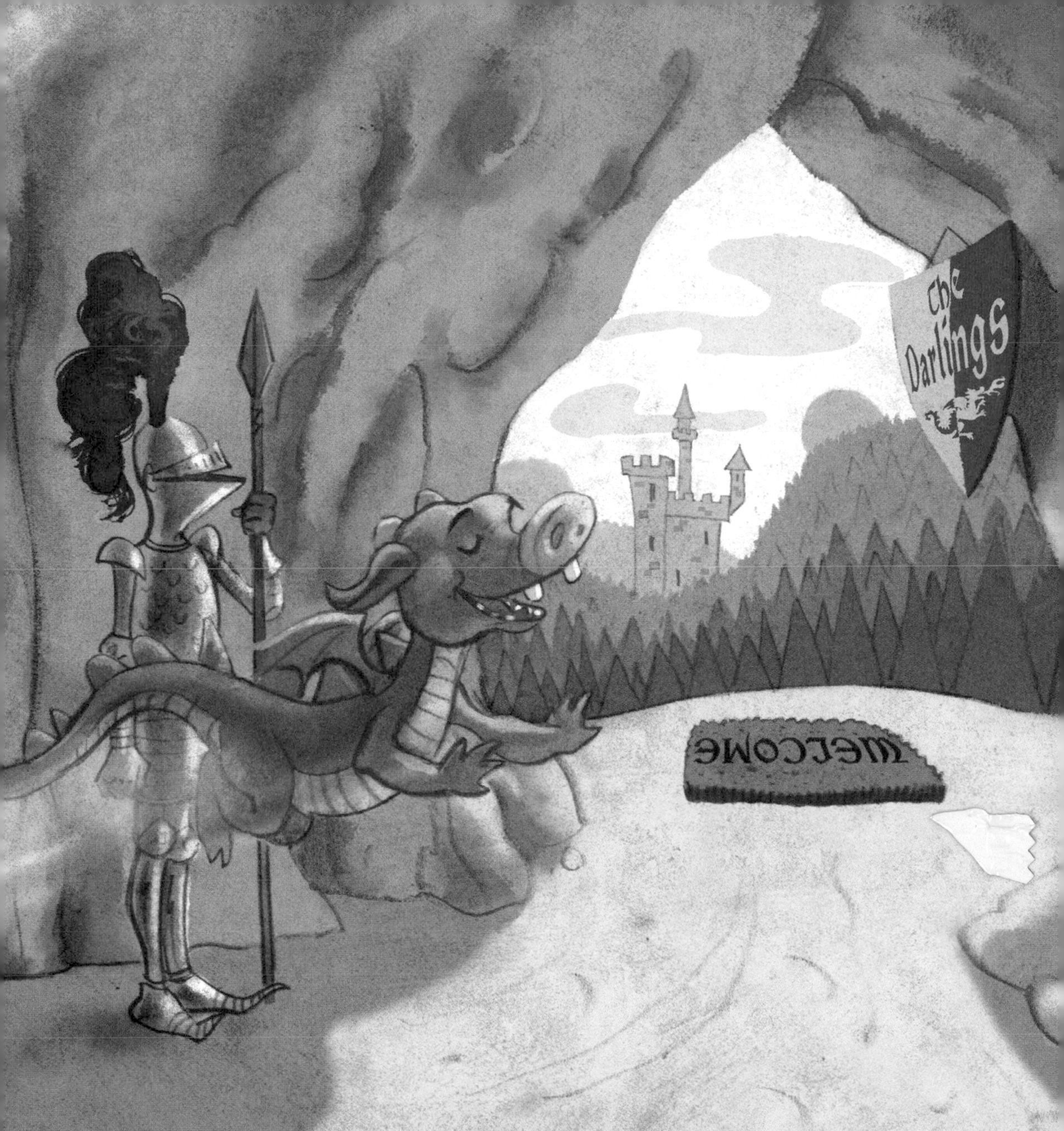

Before little dragons go to bed, they like to . . .

ROAR!

Little dragons also like to . . .

breathe **FIRE!**

Most of all, little dragons like to FLY!

But all little dragons eventually get sleepy.

So they pick up
their messes.

They put away their toys.

They brush their fangs.

They take a bath.

They dry off their scales.

Then little dragons get
into their favorite pajamas.

Finally, they climb into bed.

They get a hug and a good-night kiss from Mom and Dad.

Little dragons take a great big stretch.

Then they tuck their noses under their wings
and go to sleep.

But wait!

Little dragons can't
sleep without a night-light.

Good night, little dragons.